Anonymous

Joseph

The Hebrew prince of Egypt

Anonymous

Joseph
The Hebrew prince of Egypt

ISBN/EAN: 9783337331573

Printed in Europe, USA, Canada, Australia, Japan

Cover: Foto ©Andreas Hilbeck / pixelio.de

More available books at **www.hansebooks.com**

JOSEPH:

THE HEBREW PRINCE OF EGYPT.

BIBLE LANGUAGE.

Nine Jllustrations.

PHILADELPHIA:

PRESBYTERIAN PUBLICATION COMMITTEE,

1334 CHESTNUT STREET.

NEW YORK: A. D. F. RANDOLPH & CO., 770 BROADWAY.

How many changes Joseph passed
   Before he thirty years had known !—
He's now a slave in prison cast,
   And now exalted next the throne.

From his example may we learn
   Our various duties to fulfill,
And make it our supreme concern
   To please the Lord and do his will.

JOSEPH.

JACOB dwelt in the land wherein his father was a stranger, in the land of Canaan.

Joseph, being seventeen years old, was feeding the flock with his brethren; and Joseph brought unto his father their evil report. Now Israel loved Joseph more than all his children, because he was the son of his old age; and he made him a coat of many colors. And when his brethren saw that their father loved him more than all his brethren, they hated him, and could not speak peaceably unto him.

And Joseph dreamed a dream, and he told it his brethren; and they hated him yet the more. And he said unto them, Hear, I pray you, this dream which I have dreamed: For, behold, we were binding sheaves in the field, and, lo, my sheaf arose, and also stood upright; and, behold, your sheaves stood round about, and made obeisance to my sheaf.

And his brethren said to him, Shalt thou indeed reign over us? or shalt thou indeed have dominion over us? And they hated him yet the more for his dreams, and for his words.

And he dreamed yet another dream, and told it his brethren, and said, Behold, I have dreamed a dream more; and, behold, the sun and the moon and the eleven stars made obeisance to me. And he told it to his father,

Joseph telling his Dream.

and to his brethren; and his father rebuked him, and said unto him, What is this dream that thou hast dreamed? Shall I and thy mother and thy brethren indeed come to bow down ourselves to thee to the earth?

And his brethren envied him; but his father observed the saying.

And his brethren went to feed their father's flock in Shechem. And Israel said unto Joseph, Do not thy brethren feed the flock in Shechem? come, and I will send thee unto them. And he said to him, Here am I. And he said to him, Go, I pray thee, see whether it be well with thy brethren, and well with the flocks; and bring me word again. So he sent him out of the vale of Hebron, and he came to Shechem.

And a certain man found him, and, behold, he was wandering in the field;

and the man asked him, saying, What seekest thou?

And he said, I seek my brethren: tell me, I pray thee, where they feed their flocks.

And the man said, They are departed hence; for I heard them say, Let us go to Dothan.

And Joseph went after his brethren, and found them in Dothan. And when they saw him afar off, even before he came near unto them, they conspired against him to slay him. And they said one to another, Behold, this dreamer cometh. Come now therefore, and let us slay him, and cast him into some pit, and we will say, Some evil beast hath devoured him; and we shall see what will become of his dreams. And Reuben heard it, and he delivered him out of their hands;

and said, Let us not kill him. And
Reuben said unto them, Shed no blood,
but cast him into this pit that is in the
wilderness, and lay no hand upon him;
that he might rid him out of their
hands, to deliver him to his father
again.

And it came to pass, when Joseph
was come unto his brethren, that they
stripped Joseph out of his coat, his
coat of many colors that was on him;
and they took him, and cast him into
a pit; and the pit was empty, there
was no water in it. And they sat
down to eat bread. And they lifted up
their eyes and looked, and, behold, a
company of Ishmaelites came from
Gilead, with their camels bearing
spicery and balm and myrrh, going to
carry it down to Egypt.

And Judah said unto his brethren,

What profit is it if we slay our brother, and conceal his blood? Come, and let us sell him to the Ishmaelites, and let not our hand be upon him; for he is our brother and our flesh; and his brethren were content.

Then there passed by Midianites merchantmen; and they drew and lifted up Joseph out of the pit, and sold Joseph to the Ishmaelites for twenty pieces of silver: and they brought Joseph into Egypt.

And Reuben returned unto the pit; and, behold, Joseph was not in the pit; and he rent his clothes. And he returned unto his brethren, and said, The child is not; and I, whither shall I go? And they took Joseph's coat, and killed a kid of the goats, and dipped the coat in the blood; and they sent the coat of many colors,

Joseph sold to the Merchants.

and they brought it to their father; and said, This have we found: know now whether it be thy son's coat or no.

And he knew it, and said, It is my son's coat; an evil beast hath devoured him; Joseph is without doubt rent in pieces. And Jacob rent his clothes, and put sackcloth upon his loins, and mourned for his son many days. And all his sons and all his daughters rose up to comfort him; but he refused to be comforted; and he said, For I will go down into the grave unto my son mourning. Thus his father wept for him. And the Midianites sold him into Egypt unto Potiphar, an officer of Pharaoh's, and captain of the guard.

And Joseph was brought down to Egypt; and Potiphar, an officer of Pharaoh, captain of the guard, an

2

Egyptian, bought him of the hands of the Ishmaelites, which had brought him down thither. And the Lord was with Joseph, and he was a prosperous man; and he was in the house of his master the Egyptian. And his master saw that the Lord was with him, and that the Lord made all that he did to prosper in his hand. And Joseph found grace in his sight, and he served him: and he made him overseer over his house, and .all that he had he put into his hand. And it came to pass from the time that he had made him overseer in his house, and over all that he had, that the Lord blessed the Egyptian's house for Joseph's sake; and the blessing of the Lord was upon all that he had in the house and in the field. And he left all that he had in Joseph's hand; and he knew not aught he had, save the bread which he did eat. And Joseph was a goodly person, and well-favored.

And it came to pass after these things, that his master's wife cast her eyes upon Joseph; and she said, Lie with me. But he refused, and said unto his master's wife, Behold, my master wotteth not what is with me in the house, and he hath committed all that he hath to my hand; there is none greater in this house than I; neither hath he kept back anything from me but thee, because thou art his wife; how then can I do this great wickedness, and sin against God?

And it came to pass, as she spake to Joseph day by day, that he hearkened not unto her, to lie by her, or to be with her. And it came to pass about this time, that Joseph went into the house to do his business; and there was none of the men of the house there within. And she caught him by his garment, saying, Lie with me; and he left his garment in her hand, and fled, and got him out. And it came to pass, when she saw that he had left his garment in her hand, and was fled forth, that she called unto the men of her house, and spake unto them, saying, See, he hath brought in a Hebrew unto us to mock us; he came in unto me to lie with me, and I cried with a loud voice; and it came to pass, when he heard that I lifted up my voice and cried, that he left his garment with me, and fled, and got him out. And she laid up his garment by her, until his lord came home.

And she spake unto him according to these words, saying, The Hebrew servant, which thou hast brought unto us came in unto me to mock me; and it came to pass, as I lifted up my voice and cried, that he left his garment with me, and fled out. And it came to pass, when his master heard the words of his wife, which she spake unto him, saying, After this manner did thy servant to me, that his wrath was kindled. And Joseph's master took him, and put him into the prison, a place where the king's prisoners were bound; and he was there in the prison.

But the Lord was with Joseph, and showed him mercy, and gave him favor in the sight of the keeper of the prison. And the keeper of the prison committed to Joseph's hand all the prisoners that were in the prison; and whatsoever they did there, he was the doer of it. The keeper of the prison

2 *

looked not to anything that was under his hand; because the Lord was with him, and that which he did the Lord made it to prosper.

And it came to pass after these things, that the butler of the king of Egypt and his baker had offended their lord the king of Egypt. And Pharaoh was wroth against two of his officers, against the chief of the butlers, and against the chief of the bakers. And he put them in ward in the house of the captain of the guard, into the prison, the place where Joseph was bound. And the captain of the guard charged Joseph with them, and he served them; and they continued a season in ward.

And they dreamed a dream both of them, each man his dream in one night, each man according to the in-

terpretation of his dream, the butler
and the baker of the king of Egypt,
which were bound in the prison.

And Joseph came in unto them in
the morning, and looked upon them,
and, behold, they were sad. And he
asked Pharaoh's officers that were
with him in the ward of his lord's
house, saying, Wherefore look ye so
sadly to day?

And they said unto him, We have
dreamed a dream, and there is no interpreter of it.

And Joseph said unto them, Do not
interpretations belong to God? tell me
them, I pray you.

And the chief butler told his dream
to Joseph, and said to him, In my
dream, behold, a vine was before me;
and in the vine were three branches;
and it was as though it budded, and

Joseph in Prison.

her blossoms shot forth; and the clusters thereof brought forth ripe grapes, and Pharaoh's cup was in my hand; and I took the grapes, and pressed them into Pharaoh's cup, and I gave the cup into Pharaoh's hand.

And Joseph said unto him, This is the interpretation of it: The three branches are three days: yet within three days shall Pharaoh lift up thine head, and restore thee unto thy place; and thou shalt deliver Pharaoh's cup into his hand, after the former manner when thou wast his butler. But think on me when it shall be well with thee, and show kindness, I pray thee, unto me, and make mention of me unto Pharaoh, and bring me out of this house; for indeed I was stolen away out of the land of the Hebrews; and here also have I done nothing that they should put me into the dungeon.

When the chief baker saw that the interpretation was good, he said unto Joseph, I also was in my dream, and, behold, I had three white baskets on my head; and in the uppermost basket there was of all manner of bakemeats for Pharaoh; and the birds did eat them out of the basket upon my head.

And Joseph answered and said, This is the interpretation thereof: The three baskets are three days: yet within three days shall Pharaoh lift up thy head from off thee, and shall hang thee on a tree; and the birds shall eat thy flesh from off thee.

And it came to pass the third day, which was Pharaoh's birth-day, that he made a feast unto all his servants;

and he lifted up the head of the chief butler and of the chief baker among his servants. And he restored the chief butler unto his butlership again, and he gave the cup into Pharaoh's hand; but he hanged the chief baker; as Joseph had interpreted to them. Yet did not the chief butler remember Joseph, but forgat him.

And it came to pass at the end of two full years, that Pharaoh dreamed; and, behold, he stood by the river. And, behold, there came up out of the river seven well-favored kine and fat-fleshed; and they fed in a meadow. And, behold, seven other kine came up after them out of the river, ill-favored and lean-fleshed; and stood by the other kine upon the brink of the river. And the ill-favored and lean-fleshed kine did eat up the seven well-favored and fat kine. So Pharaoh awoke.

And he slept and dreamed the second time; and, behold, seven ears of corn came up upon one stalk, rank and good. And, behold, seven thin ears and blasted with the east wind sprung up after them. And the seven thin ears devoured the seven rank and full ears. And Pharaoh awoke, and, behold, it was a dream. And it came to pass in the morning that his spirit was troubled; and he sent and called for all the magicians of Egypt, and all the wise men thereof; and Pharaoh told them his dream; but there was none that could interpret them unto Pharaoh.

Then spake the chief butler unto Pharaoh, saying, I do remember my faults this day: Pharaoh was wroth with his servants, and put me in ward in the captain of the guard's house, both me and the chief baker; and we dreamed a dream in one night, I and he; we dreamed each man according to the interpretation of his dream. And there was there with us a young man, a Hebrew, servant to the captain of the guard; and we told him, and he interpreted to us our dreams; to each man according to his dream he did interpret. And it came to pass, as he interpreted to us, so it was; me he restored unto mine office, and him he hanged.

Then Pharaoh sent and called Joseph, and they brought him hastily out of the dungeon; and he shaved himself, and changed his raiment, and came in unto Pharaoh. And Pharaoh said unto Joseph, I have dreamed a

3

dream, and there is none that can interpret it; and I have heard say of thee, that thou canst understand a dream to interpret it. And Joseph answered Pharaoh, saying, It is not in me; God shall give Pharaoh an answer of peace.

And Pharaoh said unto Joseph, In my dream, behold, I stood upon the bank of the river; and, behold, there came up out of the river seven kine, fat-fleshed and well-favored; and they fed in a meadow; and, behold, seven other kine came up after them, poor and very ill-favored and lean-fleshed, such as I never saw in all the land of Egypt for badness; and the lean and the ill-favored kine did eat up the first seven fat kine; and when they had eaten them up, it could not be known that they had eaten them; but they

were still ill-favored, as at the begin-
ning. So I awoke. And I saw in my
dream, and, behold, seven ears came
up in one stalk, full and good; and,
behold, seven ears, withered, thin,
and blasted with the east wind, sprung
up after them; and the thin ears devoured the seven good ears; and I
told this unto the magicians; but
there was none that could declare it to
me.

And Joseph said unto Pharaoh,
The dream of Pharaoh is one: God
hath showed Pharaoh what he is
about to do. The seven good kine
are seven years; and the seven good
ears are seven years; the dream is
one. And the seven thin and ill-favored kine that came up after them
are seven years; and the seven empty
ears blasted with the east wind shall

be seven years of famine. This is the thing which I have spoken unto Pharaoh; what God is about to do he showeth unto Pharaoh. Behold, there come seven years of great plenty throughout all the land of Egypt; and there shall arise after them seven years of famine; and all the plenty shall be forgotten in the land of Egypt; and the famine shall consume the land; and the plenty shall not be known in the land by reason of that famine following; for it shall be very grievous. And for that the dream was doubled unto Pharaoh twice; it is because the thing is established by God, and God will shortly bring it to pass.

Now therefore let Pharaoh look out a man discreet and wise, and set him over the land of Egypt. Let Pharaoh

Joseph interpreting Pharach's Dream.

3 *

do this, and let him appoint officers over the land, and take up the fifth part of the land of Egypt in the seven plenteous years. And let them gather all the food of those good years that come, and lay up corn under the hand of Pharaoh, and let them keep food in the cities. And that food shall be for store to the land against the seven years of famine, which shall be in the land of Egypt; that the land perish not through the famine.

And the thing was good in the eyes of Pharaoh, and in the eyes of all his servants. And Pharaoh said unto his servants, Can we find such a one as this is, a man in whom the spirit of God is? And Pharaoh said unto Joseph, Forasmuch as God hath showed thee all this, there is none so discreet and wise as thou art: thou shalt be over my house, and according unto thy word shall all my people be ruled; only in the throne will I be greater than thou. And Pharaoh said unto Joseph, See, I have set thee over all the land of Egypt. And Pharaoh took off his ring from his hand, and put it upon Joseph's hand, and arrayed him in vestures of fine linen, and put a gold chain about his neck; and he made him to ride in the second chariot which he had; and they cried before him, Bow the knee; and he made him ruler over all the land of Egypt. And Pharaoh said unto Joseph, I am Pharaoh, and without thee shall no man lift up his hand or foot in all the land of Egypt. And Pharaoh called Joseph's name Zaphnath-paaneah; and he gave him to wife Asenath the daughter of Poti-pherah priest of On.

And Joseph went out over all the land of Egypt.

And Joseph was thirty years old when he stood before Pharaoh king of Egypt. And Joseph went out from the presence of Pharaoh, and went` throughout all the land of Egypt.

And in the seven plenteous years the earth brought forth by handfuls. And he gathered up all the food of the seven years, which were in the land of Egypt, and laid up the food in the cities; the food of the field, which was round about every city, laid he up in the same. And Joseph gathered corn as the sand of the sea, very much, until he left numbering; for it was without number.

And unto Joseph were born two sons before the years of famine came;

which Asenath the daughter of Potipherah priest of On bare unto him. And Joseph called the name of the first-born Manasseh; For God, said he, hath made me forget all my toil, and all my father's house. And the name of the second called he Ephraim; For God hath caused me to be fruitful in the land of my affliction.

And the seven years of plenteousness, that was in the land of Egypt, were ended. And the seven years of dearth began to come, according as Joseph had said; and the dearth was in all lands; but in all the land of Egypt there was bread. And when all the land of Egypt was famished, the people cried to Pharaoh for bread; and Pharaoh said unto all the Egyptians, Go unto Joseph; what he saith to you, do. And the famine was over

all the face of the earth; and Joseph
opened all the store-houses, and sold
unto the Egyptians; and the famine
waxed sore in the land of Egypt.
And all countries came into Egypt to
Joseph for to buy corn; because that
the famine was so sore in all lands.

Now when Jacob saw that there was
corn in Egypt, Jacob said unto his
sons, Why do ye look one upon
another? And he said, Behold, I
have heard that there is corn in Egypt;
get you down thither, and buy for us
from thence; that we may live, and
not die. And Joseph's ten brethren
went down to buy corn in Egypt.
But Benjamin, Joseph's brother, Jacob
sent not with his brethren; for he
said, Lest peradventure mischief befall him. And the sons of Israel
came to buy corn among those that

Joseph advanced to Honor

came; for the famine was in the land
of Canaan. And Joseph was the
governor over the land, and he it was
that sold to all the people of the land;
and Joseph's brethren came and bowed
down themselves before him with their
faces to the earth.

And Joseph saw his brethren, and
he knew them, but made himself
strange unto them, and spake roughly
unto them; and he said unto them,
Whence come ye? And they said,
From the land of Canaan to buy food.
And Joseph knew his brethren, but
they knew not him. And Joseph
remembered the dreams which he
dreamed of them, and said unto them,
Ye are spies; to see the nakedness of
the land ye are come.

And they said unto him, Nay, my
lord, but to buy food are thy servants

come. We are all one man's sons; we are true men, thy servants are no spies.

And he said unto them, Nay, but to see the nakedness of the land ye are come.

And they said, Thy servants are twelve brethren, the sons of one man in the land of Canaan; and, behold, the youngest is this day with our father, and one is not.

And Joseph said unto them, That is it that I spake unto you, saying, Ye are spies. Hereby ye shall be proved; by the life of Pharaoh ye shall not go forth hence, except your youngest brother come hither. Send one of you, and let him fetch your brother, and ye shall be kept in prison, that your words may be proved, whether there be any truth in you; or else by

4

the life of Pharaoh surely ye are spies.
And he put them all together into
ward three days.

And Joseph said unto them the
third day, This do, and live; for I
fear God: if ye be true men, let one
of your brethren be bound in the
house of your prison; go ye, carry
corn for the famine of your houses;
but bring your youngest brother unto
me; so shall your words be verified,
and ye shall not die. And they did
so.

And they said one to another, We
are verily guilty concerning our
brother, in that we saw the anguish
of his soul, when he besought us, and
we would not hear; therefore is this
distress come upon us. And Reuben
answered them, saying, Spake I not
unto you, saying, Do not sin against

the child; and ye would not hear? therefore, behold, also his blood is required. And they knew not that Joseph understood them; for he spake unto them by an interpreter. And he turned himself about from them, and wept; and returned to them again, and communed with them, and took from them Simeon, and bound him before their eyes.

Then Joseph commanded to fill their sacks with corn, and to restore every man's money into his sack, and to give them provision for the way; and thus did he unto them. And they laded their asses with the corn, and departed thence. And as one of them opened his sack to give his ass provender in the inn, he espied his money; for, behold, it was in his sack's mouth. And he said unto his brethren,

My money is restored; and, lo, it is
even in my sack; and their heart
failed them, and they were afraid,
saying one to another, What is this
that God hath done unto us?

And they came unto Jacob their
father unto the land of Canaan, and
told him all that befell unto them;
saying, The man, who is the lord of
the land, spake roughly to us, and
took us for spies of the country. And
we said unto him, We are true men;
we are no spies: we be twelve brethren, sons of our father; one is not,
and the youngest is this day with our
father in the land of Canaan. And
the man, the lord of the country, said
unto us, Hereby shall I know that ye
are true men; leave one of your
brethren here with me, and take food
for the famine of your households, and

be gone; and bring your youngest brother unto me; then shall I know that ye are no spies, but that ye are true men; so will I deliver you your brother, and ye shall traffic in the land. And it came to pass as they emptied their sacks, that, behold, every man's bundle of money was in his sack; and when both they and their father saw the bundles of money, they were afraid.

And Jacob their father said unto them, Me have ye bereaved of my children; Joseph is not, and Simeon is not, and ye will take Benjamin away; all these things are against me.

And Reuben spake unto his father, saying, Slay my two sons, if I bring him not to thee; deliver him into my hand, and I will bring him to thee again.

4 *

And he said, My son shall not go down with you; for his brother is dead, and he is left alone; if mischief befall him by the way in the which ye go, then shall ye bring down my gray hairs with sorrow to the grave.

And the famine was sore in the land. And it came to pass, when they had eaten up the corn which they had brought out of Egypt, their father said unto them, Go again, buy us a little food. And Judah spake unto him, saying, The man did solemnly protest unto us, saying, Ye shall not see my face, except your brother be with you. If thou wilt send our brother with us, we will go down and buy thee food; but if thou wilt not send him, we will not go down; for the man said unto us, Ye shall not see my face, except your brother be with you.

And Israel said, Wherefore dealt ye so ill with me as to tell the man whether ye had yet a brother? And they said, The man asked us straitly of our state, and of our kindred, saying, Is your father yet alive? have ye another brother? and we told him according to the tenor of these words. Could we certainly know that he would say, Bring your brother down? And Judah said unto Israel his father, Send the lad with me, and we will arise and go; that we may live, and not die, both we, and thou, and also our little ones. I will be surety for him; of my hand shalt thou require him; if I bring him not unto thee, and set him before thee, then let me bear the blame for ever; for except we had lingered, surely now we had returned this second time.

And their father Israel said unto them, If it must be so, now, do this; take of the best fruits in the land in your vessels, and carry down the man a present—a little balm, and a little honey, spices and myrrh, nuts and almonds; and take double money in your hand; and the money that was brought again in the mouth of your sacks, carry it again in your hand; peradventure it was an oversight. Take also your brother, and arise, go again unto the man; and God Almighty give you mercy before the man, that he may send away your other brother, and Benjamin. If I be bereaved of my children, I am bereaved.

And the men took that present,

and they took double money in their hand, and Benjamin; and rose up, and went down to Egypt, and stood before Joseph.

And when Joseph saw Benjamin with them, he said to the ruler of his house, Bring these men home, and slay, and make ready; for these men shall dine with me at noon. And the man did as Joseph bade; and the man brought the men into Joseph's house. And the men were afraid, because they were brought into Joseph's house; and they said, Because of the money that was returned in our sacks at the first time are we brought in; that he may seek occasion against us, and fall upon us, and take us for bondmen, and our asses. And they came near to the steward of Joseph's house, and they communed with him

at the door of the house, and said, O
sir, we came indeed down at the first
time to buy food; and it came to pass,
when we came to the inn, that we
opened our sacks, and behold, every
man's money was in the mouth of his
sack, our money in full weight; and
we have brought it again in our hand.
And other money have we brought
down in our hands to buy food; we
cannot tell who put our money in our
sacks.

And he said, Peace be to you, fear
not; your God, and the God of your
father, hath given you treasure in
your sacks; I had your money. And
he brought Simeon out unto them.

And the man brought the men into
Joseph's house, and gave them water,
and they washed their feet; and he
gave their asses provender. And they

made ready the present against Joseph
came at noon; for they heard that
they should eat bread there.

And when Joseph came home, they
brought him the present which was in
their hand into the house, and bowed
themselves to him to the earth. And
he asked them of their welfare, and
said, Is your father well, the old man
of whom ye spake? Is he yet alive?

And they answered, Thy servant
our father is in good health, he is yet
alive. And they bowed down their
heads, and made obeisance. And he
lifted up his eyes, and saw his brother
Benjamin, his mother's son, and said,
Is this your younger brother, of whom
ye spake unto me? And he said, God
be gracious unto thee, my son. And
Joseph made haste; for his bowels did
yearn upon his brother; and he sought

where to weep; and he entered into his chamber, and wept there.

And he washed his face, and went out, and refrained himself, and said, Set on bread. And they set on for him by himself, and for them by themselves, and for the Egyptians, which did eat with him, by themselves; because the Egyptians might not eat bread with the Hebrews; for that is an abomination unto the Egyptians. And they sat before him, the first-born according to his birth-right, and the youngest according to his youth; and the men marveled one at another. And he took and sent messes unto them from before him; but Benjamin's mess was five times so much as any of theirs. And they drank, and were merry with him.

And he commanded the steward of

Joseph maketh a Feast for his Brethren.

his house, saying, Fill the men's sacks with food, as much as they can carry, and put every man's money in his sack's mouth. And put my cup, the silver cup, in the sack's mouth of the youngest, and his corn-money. And he did according to the word that Joseph had spoken. As soon as the morning was light, the men were sent away, they and their asses.

And when they were gone out of the city, and not yet far off, Joseph said unto his steward, Up, follow after the men; and when thou dost over-take them, say unto them, Wherefore have ye rewarded evil for good? Is not this it in which my lord drinketh, and whereby indeed he divineth? ye have done evil in so doing. And he overtook them, and he spake unto them these same words.

And they said unto him, Wherefore saith my lord these words? God forbid that thy servants should do according to this thing. Behold, the money, which we found in our sacks' mouths, we brought again unto thee out of the land of Canaan; how then should we steal out of thy lord's house silver or gold? With whomsoever of thy servants it be found, both let him die, and we also will be my lord's bondmen.

And he said, Now also let it be according unto your words; he with whom it is found shall be my servant; and ye shall be blameless.

Then they speedily took down every man his sack to the ground, and opened every man his sack. And he searched, and began at the eldest, and left at the youngest; and the cup was found in

Benjamin's sack. Then they rent their clothes, and laded every man his ass, and returned to the city. And Judah and his brethren came to Joseph's house; for he was yet there; and they fell before him on the ground.

And Joseph said unto them, What deed is this that ye have done? wot ye not that such a man as I can certainly divine?

And Judah said, What shall we say unto my lord? what shall we speak? or how shall we clear ourselves? God hath found out the iniquity of thy servants; behold, we are my lord's servants, both we, and he also with whom the cup is found. And he said, God forbid that I should do so; but the man in whose hand the cup is found, he shall be my servant; and as for you, get you up in peace unto your father.

The Cup found in Benjamin's Sack.

5 *

Then Judah came near unto him, and said, O my lord, let thy servant, I pray thee, speak a word in my lord's ear, and let not thine anger burn against thy servant; for thou art even as Pharaoh. My lord asked his servants, saying, Have ye a father, or a brother? And we said unto my lord, We have a father, an old man, and a child of his old age, a little one; and his brother is dead, and he alone is left of his mother, and his father loveth him. And thou saidst unto thy servants, Bring him down unto me, that I may set mine eyes upon him. And we said unto my lord, The lad cannot leave his father; for if he should leave his father, his father would die. And thou saidst unto thy servants, Except your youngest brother come down with you, ye shall

see my face no more. And it came to
pass, when we came up unto thy servant my father, we told him the words
of my lord. And our father said, Go
again, and buy us a little food. And
we said, We cannot go down; if our
youngest brother be with us, then will
we go down; for we may not see the
man's face, except our youngest
brother be with us. And thy servant my father said unto us, Ye
know that my wife bare me two sons;
and the one went out from me, and I
said, Surely he is torn in pieces; and
I saw him not since; and if ye take
this also from me, and mischief befall
him, ye shall bring down my gray
hairs with sorrow to the grave. Now
therefore when I come to thy servant
my father, and the lad be not with us,
seeing that his life is bound up in the

lad's life; it shall come to pass, when he seeth that the lad is not with us, that he will die; and thy servants shall bring down the gray hairs of thy servant our father with sorrow to the grave. For thy servant became surety for the lad unto my father, saying, If I bring him not unto thee, then I shall bear the blame to my father for ever. Now therefore, I pray thee, let thy servant abide instead of the lad a bondman to my lord; and let the lad go up with his brethren. For how shall I go up to my father, and the lad be not with me? lest peradventure I see the evil that shall come on my father.

Then Joseph could not refrain himself before all them that stood by him; and he cried, Cause every man to go out from me.

Joseph maketh himself known to his Brethren.

And there stood no man with him, while Joseph made himself known unto his brethren. And he wept aloud; and the Egyptians and the house of Pharaoh heard. And Joseph said unto his brethren, I am Joseph; doth my father yet live? And his brethren could not answer him; for they were troubled at his presence. And Joseph said unto his brethren, Come near to me, I pray you. And they came near. And he said, I am Joseph your brother, whom ye sold into Egypt. Now therefore be not grieved, nor angry with yourselves, that ye sold me hither; for God did send me before you to preserve life. For these two years hath the famine been in the land; and yet there are five years, in the which there shall neither be earing nor harvest. And

God sent me before you to preserve
you a posterity in the earth, and to
save your lives by a great deliverance.
So now it was not you that sent me
hither, but God; and he hath made
me a father to Pharaoh, and lord of
all his house, and a ruler throughout
all the land of Egypt. Haste ye, and
go up to my father, and say unto him,
Thus saith thy son Joseph, God hath
made me lord of all Egypt; come
down unto me, tarry not; and thou
shalt dwell in the land of Goshen, and
thou shalt be near unto me, thou, and
thy children, and thy children's children, and thy flocks, and thy herds,
and all that thou hast; and there will I
nourish thee; for yet there are five years
of famine; lest thou, and thy household,
and all that thou hast, come to poverty.
And, behold, your eyes see, and the eyes

of my brother Benjamin, that it is my mouth that speaketh unto you. And ye shall tell my father of all my glory in Egypt, and of all that ye have seen; and ye shall haste and bring down my father hither.

And he fell upon his brother Benjamin's neck, and wept; and Benjamin wept upon his neck. Moreover he kissed all his brethren, and wept upon them; and after that his brethren talked with him.

And the fame thereof was heard in Pharaoh's house, saying, Joseph's brethren are come; and it pleased Pharaoh well, and his servants. And Pharaoh said unto Joseph, Say unto thy brethren, This do ye; lade your beasts, and go, get you unto the land of Canaan; and take your father and your households, and come unto me;

and I will give you the good of the land of Egypt, and ye shall eat the fat of the land. Now thou art commanded, this do ye; take you wagons out of the land of Egypt for your little ones, and for your wives, and bring your father, and come. Also regard not your stuff; for the good of all the land of Egypt is yours.

And the children of Israel did so; and Joseph gave them wagons, according to the commandment of Pharaoh, and gave them provision for the way. To all of them he gave each man changes of raiment; but to Benjamin he gave three hundred pieces of silver, and five changes of raiment. And to his father he sent after this manner: ten asses laden with the good things of Egypt, and ten she-asses laden with corn and bread and meat for his father by the way. So he sent his brethren away, and they departed; and he said unto them, See that ye fall not out by the way.

And they went up out of Egypt, and came into the land of Canaan, unto Jacob their father. And told him, saying, Joseph is yet alive, and he is governor over all the land of Egypt. And Jacob's heart fainted, for he believed them not. And they told him all the words of Joseph, which he had said unto them; and when he saw the wagons which Joseph had sent to carry him, the spirit of Jacob their father revived.

And Israel said, It is enough; Joseph my son is yet alive; I will go and see him before I die.

And Israel took his journey with all that he had, and came to Beer-sheba, and offered sacrifices unto the God of his father Isaac. And God spake unto Israel in the visions of the night, and said, Jacob, Jacob; and he said, Here am I. And he said, I am God, the God of thy father; fear not to go down into Egypt; for I will there make of thee a great nation. I will go down with thee into Egypt; and I will also surely bring thee up again; and Joseph shall put his hand upon thine eyes. And Jacob rose up from Beer-sheba; and the sons of Israel carried Jacob their father, and their little ones, and their wives, in the wagons which Pharaoh had sent to carry him. And they took their cattle, and their goods, which they had gotten in the land of Canaan, and came into Egypt, Jacob, and all his seed with him; his sons, and his sons'

sons with him, his daughters, and his sons' daughters, and all his seed brought he with him into Egypt.

And he sent Judah before him unto Joseph, to direct his face unto Goshen; and they came into the land of Goshen. And Joseph made ready his chariot, and went up to meet Israel his father, to Goshen, and presented himself unto him; and he fell on his neck, and wept on his neck a good while.

And Israel said unto Joseph, Now let me die, since I have seen thy face, because thou art yet alive.

And Joseph said unto his brethren, and unto his father's house, I will go up, and show Pharaoh, and say unto him, My brethren, and my father's house, which were in the land of Canaan, are come unto me; and the men are shepherds, for their trade hath been to feed cattle; and they have brought their flocks, and their herds, and all that they have. And it shall come to pass, when Pharaoh shall call you, and shall say, What is your occupation? that ye shall say, Thy servants' trade hath been about cattle from our youth even until now, both we, and also our fathers; that ye may dwell in the land of Goshen; for every shepherd is an abomination unto the Egyptians.

Then Joseph came and told Pharaoh, and said, My father and my brethren, and their flocks, and their herds, and all that they have, are come out of the land of Canaan; and, behold, they are in the land of Goshen. And he took some of his brethren, even five men, and presented them unto Pharaoh.

6 *

And Pharaoh said unto his brethren, What is your occupation?

And they said unto Pharaoh, Thy servants are shepherds, both we, and also our fathers. They said moreover unto Pharaoh, For to sojourn in the land are we come; for thy servants have no pasture for their flocks; for the famine is sore in the land of Canaan; now therefore, we pray thee, let thy servants dwell in the land of Goshen.

And Pharaoh spake unto Joseph, saying, Thy father and thy brethren are come unto thee: the land of Egypt is before thee; in the best of the land make thy father and brethren to dwell; in the land of Goshen let them dwell; and if thou knowest any men of activity among them, then make them rulers over my cattle.

And Joseph brought in Jacob his father, and set him before Pharaoh; and Jacob blessed Pharaoh.

And Pharaoh said unto Jacob, How old art thou?

And Jacob said unto Pharaoh, The days of the years of my pilgrimage are a hundred and thirty years; few and evil have the days of the years of my life been, and have not attained unto the days of the years of the life of my fathers in the days of their pilgrimage. And Jacob blessed Pharaoh, and went out from before Pharaoh.

And Joseph placed his father and his brethren, and gave them a posses·sion in the land of Egypt, in the best of the land, in the land of Rameses, as Pharaoh had commanded. And Joseph nourished his father, and his brethren, and all his father's household, with bread, according to their families.

And there was no bread in all the land; for the famine was very sore, so that the land of Egypt and all the land of Canaan fainted by reason of the famine. And Joseph gathered up all the money that was found in the land of Egypt, and in the land of Canaan, for the corn which they bought; and Joseph brought the money into Pharaoh's house. And when money failed in the land of Egypt, and in the land of Canaan, all the Egyptians came unto Joseph, and said, Give us bread; for why should we die in thy presence? for the money faileth. And Joseph said, Give your cattle; and I will give you for your cattle, if money fail. And they brought their cattle unto Joseph; and

Joseph gave them bread in exchange for horses, and for the flocks, and for the cattle of the herds, and for the asses; and he fed them with bread for all their cattle for that year. When that year was ended, they came unto him, the second year, and said unto him, We will not hide it from my lord, how that our money is spent; my lord also hath our herds of cattle; there is not aught left in the sight of my lord, but our bodies, and our lands. Wherefore shall we die before thine eyes, both we and our land? buy us and our land for bread, and we and our land will be servants unto Pharaoh; and give us seed, that we may live, and not die, that the land be not desolate.

And Joseph bought all the land of Egypt for Pharaoh; for the Egyptians sold every man his field, because the famine prevailed over them; so the land became Pharaoh's. And as for the people, he removed them to cities from one end of the borders of Egypt even to the other end thereof. Only the land of the priests bought he not; for the priests had a portion assigned them of Pharaoh, and did eat their portion which Pharaoh gave them; wherefore they sold not their lands.

Then Joseph said unto the people, Behold, I have bought you this day and your land for Pharaoh; lo, here is seed for you, and ye shall sow the land. And it shall come to pass in the increase, that ye shall give the fifth part unto Pharaoh, and four parts shall be your own, for seed of the field, and for your food, and for them of your households, and for food for your little ones. And they said,

Thou hast saved our lives; let us find grace in the sight of my lord, and we will be Pharaoh's servants. And Joseph made it a law over the land of Egypt unto this day, that Pharaoh should have the fifth part; except the land of the priests only, which became not Pharaoh's.

And Israel dwelt in the land of Egypt, in the country of Goshen; and they had possessions therein, and grew, and multiplied exceedingly. And Jacob lived in the land of Egypt seventeen years; so the whole age of Jacob was a hundred forty and seven years. And the time drew nigh that Israel must die; and he called his son Joseph, and said unto him, If now I have found grace in thy sight, put, I pray thee, thy hand under my thigh, and deal kindly and truly with me. Bury me not, I pray thee, in Egypt; but I will lie with my fathers, and thou shalt carry me out of Egypt, and bury me in their burying-place. And he said, I will do as thou hast said. And he said, Swear unto me. And he sware unto him. And Israel bowed himself upon the bed's head.

And it came to pass after these things, that one told Joseph, Behold, thy father is sick; and he took with him his two sons, Manasseh and Ephraim. And one told Jacob, and said, Behold, thy son Joseph cometh unto thee; and Israel strengthened himself, and sat upon the bed.

And Jacob said unto Joseph, God Almighty appeared unto me at Luz in the land of Canaan, and blessed me, and said unto me, Behold, I will make thee fruitful, and multiply thee, and I will make of thee a multitude of people; and will give this land to thy seed after thee for an everlasting possession. And now thy two sons, Ephraim and Manasseh, which were born unto thee in the land of Egypt, before I came unto thee into Egypt, are mine; as Reuben and Simeon, they shall be mine. And thy issue, which thou begettest after them, shall be thine, and shall be called after the name of their brethren in their inheritance.

And Israel beheld Joseph's sons, and said, Who are these?

And Joseph said unto his father, They are my sons, whom God hath given me in this place.

And he said, Bring them, I pray thee, unto me, and I will bless them.

7

Now the eyes of Israel were dim for age, so that he could not see. And he brought them near unto him; and he kissed them, and embraced them. And Israel said unto Joseph, I had not thought to see thy face; and, lo, God hath showed me also thy seed.

And Joseph brought them out from between his knees, and he bowed himself with his face to the earth. And Joseph took them both, Ephraim in his right hand toward Israel's left hand, and Manasseh in his left hand toward Israel's right hand, and brought them near unto him. And Israel stretched out his right hand, and laid it upon Ephraim's head, who was the younger, and his left hand upon Manasseh's head, guiding his hands wittingly; for Manasseh was the first born.

And he blessed Joseph, and said, God, before whom my fathers Abraham and Isaac did walk, the God which fed me all my life long unto this day, the Angel which redeemed me from all evil, bless the lads; and let my name be named on them, and the name of my fathers Abraham and Isaac; and let them grow into a multitude in the midst of the earth. And when Joseph saw that his father laid his right hand upon the head of Ephraim, it displeased him; and he held up his father's hand, to remove it from Ephraim's head unto Manasseh's head. And Joseph said unto his father, Not so, my father; for this is the first born; put thy right hand upon his head.

And his father refused, and said, I know it, my son, I know it; he also shall become a people, and he also shall be great; but truly his younger brother shall be greater than he, and his seed shall become a multitude of nations. And he blessed them that day, saying, In thee shall Israel bless, saying, God make thee as Ephraim and as Manasseh; and he set Ephraim before Manasseh. And Israel said unto Joseph, Behold, I die; but God shall be with you, and bring you again unto the land of your fathers. Moreover I have given to thee one portion above thy brethren, which I took out of the hand of the Amorite with my sword and with my bow. And Jacob called unto his sons, and said, Gather yourselves together, that I may tell you that which shall befall you in the last days. And when Jacob had made an end of commanding his sons, he gathered up his feet into the bed, and yielded up the ghost, and was gathered unto his people. And Joseph fell upon his father's face, and wept upon him, and kissed him. And Joseph commanded his servants the physicians to embalm his father; and the physicians embalmed Israel. And forty days were fulfilled for him; for so are fulfilled the days of those which are embalmed; and the Egyptians mourned for him threescore and ten days.

And when the days of his mourning were past, Joseph spake unto the house of Pharaoh, saying, If now I have found grace in your eyes, speak, I pray you, in the ears of Pharaoh, saying, My father made me swear, saying, Lo, I die; in my grave which I have digged for me in the land of Canaan, there shalt thou bury me.

7 *

Now therefore let me go up, I pray thee, and bury my father, and I will come again. And Pharaoh said, Go up, and bury thy father, according as he made thee swear.

And Joseph went up to bury his father; and with him went up all the servants of Pharaoh, the elders of his house, and all the elders of the land of Egypt. And all the house of Joseph, and his brethren, and his father's house; only their little ones, and their flocks, and their herds, they left in the land of Goshen. And there went up with him both chariots and horsemen; and it was a very great company. And they came to the threshing-floor of Atad, which is beyond Jordan; and there they mourned with a great and very sore lamentation; and he made a mourning for his father seven days. And when the inhabitants of the land, the Canaanites, saw the mourning in the floor of Atad, they said, This is a grievous mourning to the Egyptians; wherefore the name of it was called Abel-mizraim, which is beyond Jordan. And his sons did unto him according as he commanded them; for his sons carried him into the land of Canaan, and buried him in the cave of the field of Machpelah, which Abraham bought with the field for a possession of a burying-place of Ephron the Hittite, before Mamre.

And Joseph returned into Egypt, he, and his brethren, and all that went up with him to bury his father, after he had buried his father. And when Joseph's brethren saw that their father was dead, they said, Joseph will peradventure hate us, and will certainly requite us all the evil which we did unto him. And they sent a messenger unto Joseph, saying, Thy father did command before he died, saying, So shall ye say unto Joseph, Forgive, I pray thee now, the trespass of thy brethren, and their sin; for they did unto thee evil; and now, we pray thee, forgive the trespass of the servants of the God of thy father. And Joseph wept when they spake unto him. And his brethren also went and fell down before his face; and they said, Behold, we be thy servants. And Joseph said unto them, Fear not; for am I in the place of God? But as for you, ye thought evil against me; but God meant it unto good, to bring to pass, as it is this day, to save much people alive. Now therefore fear ye not; I will nourish you, and your little ones.

And he comforted them, and spake kindly unto them.

And Joseph dwelt in Egypt, he, and his father's house; and Joseph lived a hundred and ten years. And Joseph saw Ephraim's children of the third generation; the children also of Machir the son of Manasseh were brought up upon Joseph's knees. And Joseph said unto his brethren, I die; and God will surely visit you, and bring you out of this land unto the land which he sware to Abraham, to Isaac and to Jacob. And Joseph took an oath of the children of Israel, saying, God will surely visit you, and ye shall carry up my bones from hence. So Joseph died, being a hundred and ten years old; and they embalmed him, and he was put in a coffin in Egypt.

www.ingramcontent.com/pod-product-compliance
Lightning Source LLC
Chambersburg PA
CBHW030005030726
47499CB00008B/2909